WHEN THE HURRICANE CAME

Other Books By Nechama Liss-Levinson

Cookie the
Seder Cat

WHEN A
Grandparent
DIES

A Kid's Own

Remembering Workbook

for Dealing with Shiva

and the Year Beyond

Nechama Liss-Levinson, Ph.D.

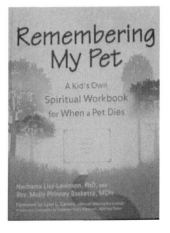

Remembering
My Pet

A Kid's Own
Spiritual Workbook
for When a Pet Dies

Nechama Liss-Levinson, Ph.D. and
Rev. Molly Phinney Baskette, MDiv

WHEN THE HURRICANE CAME

WRITTEN AND PHOTOGRAPHED BY

NECHAMA LISS-LEVINSON

ISBN: 1470082535
ISBN 13: 9781470082536

Library of Congress Control Number: 2012904898
CreateSpace, North Charleston, SC

For Marc and Sadie
& all their cousins

And for the children of New Orleans

Be the change you wish to see in the world

TABLE OF CONTENTS

CHAPTER ONE

BEFORE TROUBLE CAME TO TOWN

Before the hurricane, growing up in New Orleans was fun. I was in the fourth grade at the Jewish Academy and I knew how to read and write in both English and Hebrew, which I thought was pretty cool. I even had a copy of *The Cat in The Hat* in Hebrew, which was fun to read, even though it was a book for little kids. I loved the warm days when we had recess outside and I felt like the sun was kissing my face. I could climb higher on the outdoor gym set than anyone in my class, boys included, and on a clear day, I could see all the way to Lake Pontchartrain.

On Wednesday afternoons, Mom would take me and my brother, Jonah, to the Willow Wood

Nursing Home to visit mom's grandmother, my great grandma Rose. Wednesday was always bingo day there, and the nurses at the home let me call out the numbers, like "B 24, lucky B 24."

My brother Jonah, who's only five, would always try to copy me, but he got the numbers wrong. "B one, two, three, four," he said. I gave him my most annoying look. "Stop it Jonah," I said. "You're only mixing the old people up."

Grammy Rose loved playing bingo, and when I was there calling out the numbers, she would tell all her friends, "That's my great granddaughter Gertie calling the numbers. She's a math genius and my good luck girl." I was embarrassed and happy at the same time.

By the way, the name Gertie is my real name, not a nickname or short for anything. I was named for my grandmother, Gertrude, who died of cancer before I was born. Mom thought that Gertrude would have liked the name Gertie for me. I like it a whole lot better than "Giselle," which was the other name starting with the letter "g" that my parents were considering. There aren't any other girls named Gertie in my whole school. I think it makes me special. I also like the sound of my dad saying, "Good girl

Gertie," which, by the way, is called alliteration, when all the first letters are the same.

Anyway, enough about my name. I want to continue with my story of what life used to be like here in New Orleans. Every Thursday, after school, I took voice lessons. My hobby was singing and I had memorized all the words to Louis Armstrong's song, "What A Wonderful World," which is not so surprising in New Orleans where jazz is everyone's favorite music. I sang the song all the time, till my brother Jonah said it was giving him a headache and could I just stop it.

And Saturday morning, without fail, my mom and dad took my brother and me to services at Congregation Beth Israel. We would join the prayers at the Junior Congregation and then we would hang around to kiss the Torahs when they came out of the ark, and after services, we would eat cookies and sponge cake at the Kiddush. (A Kiddush is like a party at the synagogue with people and food, but it doesn't have to be anyone's birthday.)

Sometimes, when I was feeling brave, bored and a little bit bad, Jonah and I would sneak into the Kiddush room and eat a rainbow cookie or two before the morning services were even over. Jonah was just following me, copying me as usual. It was never his idea to sneak the cookies, and a couple of times I had to explain to him that he couldn't tell everyone what we were doing. It was a secret. But we never got in trouble for eating those cookies, and boy were they delicious!

That's how it used to be before August 29, 2005. That's the day when Hurricane Katrina came to New Orleans. Since that day, nothing has ever been the same.

CHAPTER TWO

PACKING PROBLEMS

On Sunday August 28th, my mom woke us up early and said we had to leave town. There was a big hurricane coming and we would have to get out of New Orleans for a couple of days till the storm passed over. We should pack two days of clothing and some books or toys to take to my Aunt Charlene's house, which is in Memphis, Tennessee. I was in a bad mood that day, because I wanted to go to my friend Sadie's swimming pool birthday party in her backyard, and instead there we were having to pack our stuff and get in the car to drive for five hours.

We had been through hurricanes before, and at least three times that I could remember, we had packed up to visit Aunt Charlene, her husband, Uncle Mike and their baby Sam. It was no big deal and I knew what to do. It was just annoying.

"OK, OK. I know we're in a rush. I am packing and I'll be ready in a couple of minutes. I can't go any faster." That's me acting up, as my dad would say. I can admit now that I was acting a little bratty, and not using the nicest manners that I had been taught. Looking back, I'm sure that it was probably an annoying day for my mom too. But she kept repeating herself about how we had to get ready and go soon. "OK, OK already," I thought to myself.

I packed my navy sweatpants and my New Orleans Saints sweatshirt. I also packed a "Save Darfur" t-shirt and some shorts and underwear. I was wearing my flip flops, and didn't feel like packing any shoes, because they are just so heavy, and I knew I would have to carry my suitcase to the car myself. I threw in two books from the library I hadn't read yet, both of them from the Lemony Snicket collection, *A Series of Unfortunate Events*. I added my toothbrush, my hairbrush, two headbands and that seemed like plenty.

I didn't realize when I was packing that I would never see any of my clothes or books or toys again. If I had known that, I would have packed my favorite jeans, my gold and black fancy dress that I wore to my Aunt Charlene's wedding, and probably, I would have packed my shoes even though they were heavy (including: my best sneakers, my green boots, my black patent leather shoes with the gold bows, and my fuzzy purple slippers).

I would have taken my collection of Barbie dolls, my computer (really it's our family computer, but I definitely would have taken it with me), my CDs which included all of Louis Armstrong's songs, and the DVDs of my favorite movies, especially *The Sound of Music*. I would have taken my stuffed animals, my glass animal collection, and my favorite board games, including Clue, which I'm really good at. I would have taken every single book I own, including the entire *Baby-Sitters Club* series, the *All-of-a Kind Family* book collection, my Siddur from first grade, and of course, all of my *Harry Potter* books.

But I didn't know what was going to happen in the future when I was packing my bag. And so, when the hurricane came, we lost everything that was in our house that we didn't take with us that morning. And it's hard to understand, but I mean everything.

Everyone says we're so lucky that we left New Orleans in time, and we weren't stuck in the house or anything. I mean, I know it's really lucky we weren't sleeping in our beds upstairs and we weren't drowned by the rains, like some people were. Also, we were lucky that we had a nice place to sleep at Aunt Charlene and Uncle Mike's house, and that we had food to eat, and there was electricity for us to use. But boy, I sure didn't feel lucky at the time. I worried all the time about our house, and about my school and my friends and about what would happen next.

I was also worried about my dad. He was a doctor at a hospital in New Orleans, and he didn't leave when we did. He stayed to help his patients there. And after the first night, we couldn't speak to him because there was no electricity in his hospital, and his cell phone stopped working. And no other phones in the city were working either. In Memphis, my mom kept calling his number every half hour or so. When nobody answered, my mom would start to cry.

Then my Aunt Charlene would put her arm around her, and say, "Jill, I'm sure Marc is fine. He's just a hero helping half of humanity."

I bit my lip and didn't say anything every time Aunt Charlene said that. On the one hand, it sounded like a good thing, and I was proud of my dad. On the other hand, what did she actually mean, "helping half of humanity?" I wasn't even sure what it meant, and anyway, I wanted him here with us in Memphis.

CHAPTER THREE

WATCHING TV ISN'T ALWAYS FUN

My mom and my Aunt Charlene kept changing their minds about whether we should watch the news on TV or not. At first, it didn't seem so bad. It looked like every other hurricane to me. But then, the next day, the gates holding back the waters of the river broke apart and the whole city began to be flooded. Those gates are called "levees," and when the levees broke, everything changed and the world outside seemed upside down. We began to see weird things on the TV screen. People were going down the streets in boats. Some people were sitting on their rooftops, with the water all around them, looking like they were in a disaster movie.

There were dogs and cats with no food and no people to feed them. The people who owned them had to leave quickly, just like we did, and many people couldn't take their pets with them, especially if they had to leave on buses or had no room in their cars. Babies were crying and some people said they needed some medicine, but there were no stores open. Cars were floating in the water and people had to travel in boats down their streets. After that news story, my mom turned the TV off for a while and said we should read the books we had brought with us.

But we saw some good things on the TV too. They showed police officers who were rescuing people from the rooftops with helicopters. That seemed pretty cool. They showed doctors in hospitals with new little babies who were really cute. Every time they showed a hospital, we would call out to my mom, and she came running in to see if my dad was on the TV.

"Mom," Jonah would scream. "Mom, I see Daddy. Daddy's on TV." But Jonah didn't know what he was talking about. Every time he saw a doctor, he thought it was Dad. This got very nerve wracking.

"Stop it Jonah," I said, in my know-it-all big sister voice. "Not every doctor on TV is Daddy. You are making us all more upset."

Jonah looked at me. He didn't start crying, which is probably what I would have done if someone spoke to me in that tone of voice. Instead, he just acted like he was the person who was older and knew what was right.

"Mom," he said. "Mom, I see Daddy. Daddy's on TV."

I looked, but it wasn't our dad.

But one time, we did see our synagogue on the TV. At first, I didn't know what was happening. They showed the building, which I knew was our synagogue, with the big Jewish stars, and the sign "Congregation Beth Israel." But the next part of the news story was weird. Inside, the synagogue was filled with water, almost like an indoor swimming pool! Two men I didn't recognize were wearing raincoats and big boots and dashed into the synagogue to find our Torahs and rescue them from the flooding.

I had always believed that nothing could ever happen to the Torahs in our synagogue. They were kept in a beautiful Aron Kodesh, a wooden closet with all kinds of pretty stars and flowers and Hebrew words carved into the wood. I never imagined that they would ever be in danger or need to be rescued. I thought that they were a gift from God and that they would always be there, kind of like God, watching over and protecting me.

I knew that one of our Torahs was brought to New Orleans from a town in Poland after the Holocaust. The Polish synagogue had been burned down by the Nazis, but a brave person had grabbed the Torah out of the burning synagogue and buried it in their backyard during World War II. They had saved the Torah, and years later, it had traveled thousands of miles to be in our synagogue.

I remember how I felt when I first heard the story about this Torah that was rescued. I was so angry and confused about the Nazis wanting to destroy the synagogue and the Jewish people and so happy that the Torah had been saved. I was especially proud that the Torah was now in our synagogue in New Orleans.

Now that I was watching the news, I was a little scared. I didn't like that the synagogue looked like a swimming pool.

My mom came in to watch the show. I asked her what she thought.

"Well," she said, "we need to be grateful that this special Torah which was rescued once has survived so much, and we can be glad that it looks like it will be rescued again."

My mom tends to be very optimistic and up-beat, which is good in a lot of ways.

But what we didn't know while we were watching the TV broadcast was that this Torah that had once been buried in Poland would not survive the flood, and would have to be buried again. But that part comes later in the story.

How To Get To New Orleans From MEMPHIS, TENNESSEE

1. Find out the number for the GREYHOUND Bus Company.

2. Call the Bus Company.

3. Find out when the buses go to

CHAPTER FOUR

THE BUS TRIP I ALMOST WENT ON

It wasn't until three days later on Wednesday when I realized that it was Bingo Day at Willow Wood Nursing Home and we wouldn't be able to be there that I asked Mom about Grammy Rose. WHERE WAS SHE? I felt badly that I hadn't thought about her till then, but everything was so mixed up!

Mom told me that all the old people at Willow Wood had been put on buses to Houston, Texas. It took the nurses and the staff many hours to get all the old people out of their rooms, especially people in wheelchairs and walkers and all that stuff. It was hard getting them up on the buses, because lots of them couldn't even climb up the three steps to get on the bus. And they didn't get to pack anything at all to take with them.

Mom said it took eight hours to get all the people on the bus and almost eight more hours to get to the nursing home in Houston, where they would be staying for a while. That was really a rough trip for these old people, almost as hard as the people who went on covered wagons two or three hundred years ago. They were cold and tired and hungry, and maybe a little scared too.

Some of the old people were kind of confused and weren't sure where they were, and it was hard to find everyone's relatives to let them know that they were safe in Texas now. Mom promised that we could speak to Grammy on the phone and help her not to feel scared or alone.

I asked if we could call her right away, and Mom said she couldn't see any reason why not, since the phones still worked in Houston. And so we did.

I called Grammy right then and I sang "It's a Wonderful World" to her. Once I sang my song, she knew who it was calling and said, "It's my lucky girl, Gertie, isn't it?"

This time, I was really happy. I told her we would play bingo when we all got back to New Orleans. Whenever that would be.

After speaking to Grammy Rose, I began to think more about where Dad might be and worried that we hadn't spoken to him yet. I decided that maybe I would have to go back down to New Orleans to see if I could find him.

I know that sounds kind of dumb, with me just being nine years old and all, but I felt that if all the old people could go on a bus to Houston, maybe I could go on a bus to New Orleans. I had to plan it out carefully, because the phones to New Orleans still weren't working and I knew in my heart my mom wouldn't like the idea all that much. Even though she's an optimist, she worries about her kids.

I needed a plan. So I got out a yellow pad from my Aunt Charlene's desk, and I made a list.

HOW TO GET TO NEW ORLEANS FROM MEMPHIS, TENNESSEE

1. Find out the telephone number for the Greyhound Bus Company.
2. Call the bus company.

3.   Find out when the buses go to New Orleans and how much they cost.
4.   Pack a snack.
5.   Pack pjs, underwear, toothbrush and a book.
6.   Write a note to Mom, explaining everything.

The first thing I did was number one on my list. I found out the number of the bus company from the operator. You can do that by calling 411 on the telephone. That was very easy.

Then, I put a line through the number one on my list. I've seen my mom do that, and I know she loves "crossing things off the list". I thought it was OK, nothing special. But now I was up to number two.

I used the phone number to call the Greyhound Bus Company, which has buses that go everywhere. It was hard to get to speak to anyone on the phone. Instead, every time I called, a voice on a machine would come on and ask me questions, like "Would you like to travel in the next twenty-four hours or in the next week?" I wasn't always sure of the answer, and then the lady on the voice machine would hang up before I could ask my questions. But I kept trying and trying, and finally, I spoke to someone and not just a voice answering machine.

I was pretty upset when after all the work I had done to speak to her, this lady said to me, "What are you thinking? There are no buses going down to New Orleans now! How old are you anyhow, and where's your mother?"

I was pretty surprised that there were no buses going to New Orleans, because Greyhound has advertisements that they always have buses going places. Also, I was very annoyed that she asked me how old I was. After all, Grammy Rose went on a bus and she's over ninety. Why can't I go on a bus when I'm already nine years old?

Anyway, it seemed the Greyhound thing wasn't going to work, so I asked Aunt Charlene if I could use her computer for some research I was doing. Aunt Charlene is extremely nice.

"Research?" she asked with a smile.

"Sure thing Gertie. I'll be finished using the computer in a minute."

So then, I went online to try to find out another way to get to New Orleans. When I typed in "NOLA," short for New Orleans, Louisiana, the worst stories I had ever seen came up on the computer.

For example, some of those pets that didn't get food were now dead. I began crying now.

I really wanted to see my dad and make sure he was OK, and not sick or dying like the dogs and cats we had seen. I was trying to check if there was a train to New Orleans now that Greyhound wasn't running, when my brother Jonah interrupted me on the computer to say Mom needed help bringing in some groceries from the car.

I went out to help her and boy, you never think you'll get in trouble for helping someone out, but I sure did. While I was helping Mom with the groceries, my Aunt Charlene went over to do something else on the computer and she figured out that I was trying to figure out how to get to New Orleans.

"Jill," she said, with a tense voice, talking to my mom. "I think you need to see this."

So then, while I was trying to be a "good girl Gertie" and help with the groceries, my mom goes to see what I was doing on the computer. And oh yeah, my list of things to do was sitting there next to the computer also.

The next thing I know, I'm putting away the Cheerios and I hear my mom calling me. "Gertie," she yells, kind of loudly. "Come in here this minute. What on earth do you think you are doing?"

Now Mom sounded like the lady at Greyhound and I just couldn't take it. Didn't anyone understand that I needed to go find my dad and make sure that he was OK? I tried to explain to Mom, but she just didn't seem to get it. She just kept shaking her head and saying, "What were you thinking?" And then to make it even worse, she added, "Don't you think it's hard enough for all of us already? We don't need you to be cooking up foolish schemes."

Foolish schemes? I thought I was doing something good. Sometimes, it's hard to explain, when you think you are just trying to help.

Mom went out of the room for a couple of minutes to speak to Aunt Charlene and when she came back, I saw there were some tears in her eyes. "Listen honey," she said now, and I could tell that Aunt Charlene's good qualities had helped, and maybe she hadn't thought it was such a bad thing I had done.

"I know you were trying to help out," Mom said softly now, "but we all need to work together as a team. When you have an idea, you need to come talk to me and we'll work together on these things like all teammates do. What do you think of that, Gertie?"

Well, this sure sounded better, even though it now seemed to me like my trip to New Orleans to find my dad wasn't going to happen. So I thought I should check it out with my mom, since she said we should talk about all of our new ideas.

"OK, Mom," I said. "But what about the trip to New Orleans? I think someone needs to find Dad before something really bad happens to him. And you seem to be OK here with Aunt Charlene and Uncle Mike, and Sam and Jonah, so I guess I should be the one to go find Dad."

My voice got really loud while I was talking and by the end I was kind of shouting at my mom. That was a little surprising.

Maybe it was even more surprising that she wasn't angry back at me. Instead, she seemed kind of sad and almost quiet.

"I know you're worried about Dad," Mom said. "But we have to have faith that he's OK and taking care of the sick people still in New Orleans. We're going to keep calling and hopefully, very soon we'll hear from him. Dad is pretty good at knowing how to take care of other people, but he also knows that he has to take care of himself so that he can be able take care of everyone else. NO MORE TRIPS BY YOURSELF. Is that clear, Gertie?"

So that seemed to end my solo bus trip back to New Orleans.

What I didn't know is that it would still be three more days till we talked to my dad and two more weeks till we actually saw him. Those two weeks were really long. Uncle Mike gave me a calendar, and I put an "X" through every day that passed. The only strange thing about my "X" marks was that the police in New Orleans were also putting an "X" on front doors to houses where people had drowned.

CHAPTER FIVE

MY DAD IS A REAL HERO

It was now the beginning of September, which is when school is already in session. Of course we couldn't go back to the Hebrew Academy in New Orleans, but my mom said we still needed to be educated. So we had to start school in Memphis, for now.

The Hebrew Academy in Memphis was willing to take in the Jewish kids from New Orleans, so I started the school year there. It was OK, but I felt funny. I didn't have my friends, my own room, my toys, my books, or my stuff. People from the Memphis Jewish community came to my aunt's house, and brought us boxes with toys, books and school supplies. That was really nice of the people to do, but I felt strange looking at the stuff. It didn't feel like it was mine, even thought my mom said that now it was.

Someone sent over some gift cards that you could use to go shopping and buy some clothes. That was a little more fun, kind of like it was your birthday or something. All of this felt odd to me. I remembered all of the times that we had raised money in school for people who had different problems, for the kids in the Special Olympics, for the orphans in Rwanda, for blind children in Israel. We gave tzedakah to help other people. And now people were giving tzedakah to help us. Mom said that this was a blessing we should accept, and that the day would come when we would be helping other people again.

"OK," I said. It seemed like all I ever said nowadays was "OK."

Dad finally came to see us, just like Mom had said. And just like Mom promised, he was OK. What wasn't OK was finding out that our house in New Orleans and much of our neighborhood had been totally destroyed by the hurricane. My dad was the one who brought us that news when he finally came up to see us in Memphis.

First the rains came, and then the crazy winds. The winds broke most of our windows and made a giant-sized hole in our roof. Then the rains came in through the broken windows and that hole in the roof.

Afterwards the really heavy rains fell and the even crazier winds began to blow. These winds were going over one hundred miles per hour. That's faster than the fastest car you've ever been in. It might be faster than any train too. These winds broke the levees, which were like gates holding back Lake Pontchartrain. And when the gates broke, then the beautiful lake began to flood the whole city, including our house. The water rushed into our house, even up to the second floor where all our bedrooms were.

Everything that was in the house was soaking wet. Every single thing. And after the hurricane was over, there was no electricity or air conditioning, just hot air and smelly water sitting for days in the house. Everything we had was ruined. Stuff that we left in the refrigerator went rotten, and the whole refrigerator smelled disgusting. Things made of paper, like books and photographs, just disintegrated and fell apart if you touched them. Stuff made of material, like your bedspread or a couch or any clothing, rotted and smelled bad and grew mold that was green and black and brown and blue.

Dad had other stories, too about what he did that you wouldn't believe.

When the electricity went out, he was still at the hospital with some nurses and some police officers. At first there were back up generators for the electricity, but then they went down too. They had to run up and down the stairs in total pitch black darkness to get food and medicine for the patients who were there. But the story I liked the best was how my dad was a hero.

Some patients needed help breathing, and used a special machine called a respirator. The respirators couldn't work without electricity, so the doctors and nurses and police had to stand by the beds of the people who needed these machines and pump air to them using their hands. My dad stood for twelve hours by one woman's bed to help her breathe. Finally, a police officer took over and my dad lay down for a couple of hours. I thought it was really cool that my dad was a real live HERO.

After he came home that first time, he kept driving back and forth from New Orleans to Memphis and back again. He'd be with us for two or three days, and then he'd be gone for a week or more. When we were lucky, he'd be with us for Shabbat. He said commuting made him realize how lucky we had all been. It didn't feel lucky to me, but I didn't say anything. I didn't want to upset either of my parents. They seemed kind of sensitive since the whole hurricane thing.

CHAPTER SIX

NEW YEAR KUGEL ADVENTURE

Rosh HaShana, the Jewish New Year, was coming soon. We weren't sure if my dad would be able to get away from the hospital to be with us. I didn't remember another Rosh HaShana that he wasn't at home with us. In the past, Dad was always with us when we heard the shofar being blown at the synagogue. I wasn't even sure how it would sound without him.

At school, my teacher said that the shofar sounds like someone crying. She asked why that might be.

I raised my hand with a smart answer. "People cry when their parents can't be with them on the holiday."

I thought it was a good answer. But then I saw some kids whispering, and I got worried. I wondered if they were whispering about me and my family. I raised my hand again and asked if I could go to the bathroom. I needed to get out before I started crying with everyone watching me.

I was getting worried about being at my Aunt Charlene and Uncle Mike's house for the holidays. I know they're trying really hard to make it "all work." Uncle Mike is always offering to play Uno with me and Candyland with Jonah. They bought these games when they found out that we were coming to stay over, which was very generous of them, because their little boy is only ten months old and can't play either of these games yet. It's also nice of Uncle Mike to play these games, because I'm not really sure he likes them (certainly not Candyland; it's so babyish) and yet he spends time playing them with us. I think he feels bad for us that Dad's not around so much. He also offers to play catch with me or Jonah, or to "do a little batting practice," which is funny because neither of us plays softball and Dad never does batting practice with us. But he's trying to be nice, for sure.

There's one room for Mom and Dad to share (when Dad gets here), and then Jonah and I share a room with baby Sam. There was a high rise bed in Sam's room before we ever got there, so there's a place for us to sleep and it's not on the floor or anything (Some of my friends have emailed me that they have to sleep in sleeping bags on the floor. The sleeping bags are cute, but the floor is a little hard.)

It's not that I really mind it. Baby Sam is totally cute. But he sometimes wakes up at night when I want to sleep, and he's sleeping at night when I want to read, so I guess you'd say we're not on the same schedule. And also, with Jonah and Sam as my roommates, I'm the only girl, two against one, which I don't really like. Even though it's hard to know whether to count Sam or not. He's not even one year old yet.

But also the food is different here. Even though my mom and Aunt Charlene are sisters, they don't cook exactly the same. It's not that I'm complaining, or that Aunt Charlene isn't a good cook, it's just that some of my favorite things are just not here.

So for example, for Shabbat dinner, Aunt Charlene made chicken with barbecue sauce, which tasted good, but not as good as my mom's chicken with "herbes de Provence" which are special French spices that my mom uses.

Now it was going to be Rosh HaShana, and at home, my mom always makes my favorite noodle pudding, called Luckshen Kugel to eat for the holiday. It was Grandma Gertrude's recipe, and so I kind of feel like it's my recipe too. Lots of Jewish families make noodle pudding, but there are also many different recipes. Some families make it salty (ughhh!) and others make it sweet (yeah!!!).

My mom's recipe also has apples and raisins stuffed inside and I think it's great. In truth, I don't really like the raisins, but it's been our family tradition that it's made that way. So now, I'm used to the raisins. I want to have them there, and then I just pick them out. Which is my way of enjoying the Luckshen Kugel and honoring my Grandma Gertrude (who, if you've followed the story, I never really met in person, but know her through eating the sweet apple-raisin noodle pudding.)

So it turns out that Aunt Charlene doesn't make this pudding for Rosh HaShana. She makes some kind of potato thing from Uncle Mike's side of the family. Mom and I were talking about Rosh HaShana and how it's going to be different this year.

"But at least we'll have the Luckshen Kugel?" I asked, smiling my cutest smile.

"Well, honey, I'm not sure," Mom said, biting her lip in her worried way. "I know Aunt Charlene wants to make everything the way we want it, but I don't want to be a burden for her. You know, she has baby Sam and her job as a lawyer and now all of us staying here......"

I knew what to expect when my mother used that voice. It was her "Let's not cause any trouble" voice. It worried me because I thought it meant no noodle pudding for Rosh HaShana.

This did not sit well with me. I understood all the things we had to give up. But did this have to be one of them? I felt sad right in my stomach.

Two nights before Rosh HaShana, we had spaghetti for dinner.

"I don't know what I was thinking. I made too many noodles," my Aunt Charlene sighed. My mind lit up like a flashlight!

I had an idea. I'd make a noodle pudding for the holiday. What a great idea. I kind of knew what to do.

When everyone was finished, I shooed them out of the kitchen. "You're all working so hard," I said. "Let me clean up."

"Wow," my mom said, really proud of me. "Thanks honey. We are all a bit tired. Do you need any help?"

"Nope," I said. "Just you all go and relax in the den and I'll be here in a couple of minutes." To tell the truth, it was easy to get them out and it didn't take much pushing.

Uncle Mike took Jonah to play Candyland. Aunt Charlene took Sam in for his bath, and my Mom went to call my Dad to check again if he would be up in Memphis for the holiday.

So this was my big chance.

I threw all the dishes into the dishwasher (I didn't exactly throw them, since they could break, but you know what I mean).

I then took all the extra spaghetti noodles and decided they would be just fine, thank-you for my kugel. I got a big glass bowl and put them in. I then added some raisins (as I told you, that's the family tradition) and a cup of sugar from the pantry. I thought my mom used to put eggs in, but the only ones I found were hard boiled, so I peeled them and put them in too, kind of squishing them up a bit. The hardest part would be the apple, because they are hard to cut. So I decided instead to put in some applesauce I found and also one whole apple in the middle, which looked very nice. I then added little cubes of margarine and here it was all done. I was ready to cook it. I'm not allowed to bake by myself, so I put it all in the microwave, which I am allowed to use (as long as you put in glass and NO metal, ever).

I set the microwave for five minutes, because I thought that would be all the time I would have till the adults would get suspicious and anyway, everyone always says things cook fast in the microwave.

When the microwave went off after five minutes, I took out my kugel. To tell the truth, it looked a little weird, with the apple sticking out of the middle, but it didn't smell at all bad. I then remembered that vanilla makes things smell good, so I got out the vanilla and added a spoon or two of that to my cooked kugel. And it did smell good.

I put lots of aluminum foil on the kugel and then wrote a sign. "This belongs to GERTIE! Don't touch it. Don't eat it. Don't even peek." And then I put it in the refrigerator.

Things began to turn around as the holiday got closer. Uncle Mike bought Jonah and me little bears filled with honey for the holiday. Those honey bears could be twins with the ones we always had at home, so I was pretty happy about that. Also, last minute, Dad was able to come up to Memphis, even though it would only be for forty-eight hours for the holiday. But at least we wouldn't have to hear the crying shofar without him.

And when it was time for the meal, I brought out my special new Gertie's Kugel.

"Tada!" I said.

"What's this?" asked everyone, including Mom, Dad, Aunt Charlene, Uncle Mike and Jonah.

"This," I said, "is our family tradition. It is Grandma Gertrude's Luckshen Kugel, with Gertie's new recipe."

They looked quite surprised. You might even say startled. But then, they all began to applaud and clap and say, "Hooray for Gertie!" I thought it was probably the best time I had had since the hurricane.

I cut a piece for everyone. Every single person except for Jonah really liked it. They all said it was "absolutely delicious." Only Jonah said, "This is disgusting, Gertie. What did you put in it?" But that's Jonah's opinion, and not any one else's.

Now, I tasted it and thought it was a little strange myself. But I think my happiness at everyone being together and being so proud of me made it taste better. I also poured some of my honey bear on it, which made it better tasting.

At that point, all Jonah could say was, "Gertie, that's really gross. The honey bear is only for apples, not for your kugel."

So I said, "Jonah, you don't know any better, because you are only a five year old chef. And I am almost ten. So I have better taste than you. Now and forever. So there. And Happy New Year to you too."

The next day, we went to my Aunt and Uncle's synagogue in Memphis. The Rabbi welcomed all the people from New Orleans. He asked us all to stand up and say a blessing together, Birkat HaGomel, thanking God for rescuing us from a dangerous situation. I was proud to say the blessing, but I didn't really feel like standing up in front of everyone. I didn't like the feeling that people were looking at me. I missed our synagogue. They didn't have rainbow cookies here, and running around with Jonah didn't seem like that much fun.

CHAPTER SEVEN

THE NOAH PROBLEM

It seemed like forever, but I finally made some new friends at my school. I had probably gotten off to a bad start. In one of the first weeks of school, the teacher, Morah Moscowitz, was talking about the Bible story about Noah. That's a story you learn every year from when you're in kindergarten, so of course all of us knew the story.

But the teacher was telling us how God had made a promise to Noah never to bring another flood like that to destroy the earth. And the rainbow is the sign of that promise, which is why everyone loves rainbows. (And maybe, I was thinking, why I love rainbow cookies so much too. It's a religious kind of thing. That was a surprise for me.)

So I was just quietly sitting at my desk, and drawing a rainbow in different colors while I was also listening, and suddenly, it hit me! If God had promised never to send another flood, what had happened in New Orleans?

I raised my hand.

"Yes, Gertie," the teacher said, with a smile and not knowing what was coming.

"Is God a liar?" I asked, not trying to be a smarty pants or a fresh kid, but just trying to figure things out.

"No Gertie, of course not!" the Morah's voice was now a little louder and not as sweet.

I didn't think she understood me. I tried again. "Does the Torah tell lies then?"

Now kids were laughing and cracking up and covering their mouths like I was saying bad things, but I wasn't. I was only trying to figure out the story with Noah and the flood and the promise of the rainbow.

"Gertie, what are you talking about?" she said, now a little snappy.

"Well, if God promised Noah that there wouldn't be another flood, then how did New Orleans get flooded by Hurricane Katrina, where people and animals died?" I just decided to ask it. "Where was the rainbow promise? Where was God?"

Now the kids were looking like I had really done something bad, or like I was a loco nut or something. Everyone stopped laughing and got real quiet.

I had a feeling like I had made a big mistake with my big mouth.

"Gertie," now the teacher's voice was quieter. "You have some big questions for a little girl."

I hate that little girl thing. I AM almost ten.

"Let's ask Rabbi Weiss to come to our class to talk about it. In the meantime, what ideas do all of you have about Noah and the flood and New Orleans?"

One boy named Joey raised his hand. Before that day, I had kind of liked Joey, because he often said things that made me laugh. But not on this day, that's for sure. Joey said he had heard that the flood came to New Orleans because the people there had done bad things, just like in the time of Noah.

Well, at that point, I had heard about enough. I jumped out of my seat and ran over to Joey. I began hitting him on the arm and on his shoulder, even though usually I don't hit people, unless you count my brother Jonah.

The next thing I knew, Morah Moscowitz was yelling "Gertie! Stop it!" at the top of her lungs and pulling me off of Joey. And then I found myself marching down to Rabbi Weiss' office.

It was strange because I have never been sent to the principal's office before in all of my years at the Hebrew Academy. And here I was in Memphis just for two weeks, and in trouble already. I was thinking that my mom and dad were NOT going to be happy. I was trying to figure out how things went so quickly from my asking a good question to my pounding Joey on the shoulder.

But as it turned out, Rabbi Weiss was a really nice rabbi. He actually understood my question about Noah and the rainbow, and he tried to explain his answer, which had something to do with the idea that God had only promised not to kill EVERYONE next time. So the fact is, in New Orleans, not everyone died, and so many people were saved and alive, so the rainbow thing was still OK. And also, he agreed that the hurricane did NOT happen because the people in New Orleans had been bad. He said we can't make those judgments. Sometimes, bad things happen to good people. I agreed.

But I still had to stay for one day's detention after school for hitting Joey. And I had to write a note to him explaining that I disagreed with his ideas about God and hurricanes, but that hitting him was not the appropriate way to show my disagreement.

And Rabbi Weiss said that I was very thoughtful, and would I like to be his assistant in writing about the weekly Torah portion for the school newspaper, and I said, "Yes indeedy Rabbi. I think that's a good idea. Thank-you very much for your offer!"

But getting back to making friends at school. I don't think that the time I called God a liar and hit Joey helped my reputation at school. And then some kids thought I was kind of like a "teacher's pet" to Rabbi Weiss after he asked me to help him with the newspaper column, but I really thought he needed help and the two of us thought a lot the same about things. I began writing down questions in a special "reporter's notebook" to discuss with him. I think I helped him a lot. He always ended our time together by saying, "Thanks Gertie. I've really learned a lot from you today." So I tried to write down questions that I thought might help him out some more.

So it was a big deal when I finally began to make some friends. There was Hannah and Rachel and Aviva and Charlie and Gabe. And even Joey and I got to be friends too. After I wrote my note to him, his parents made him write a note back saying that he had made a mistake and was sorry he had hurt my feelings. People from New Orleans, like me, seemed like regular people and were not bad. So he turned out to be a good boy to be friends with and also, like I said, he was really funny too.

They were all nice and we did stuff together, like going roller blading and going bowling and watching DVDs at someone's house. I wasn't sure if I should really try to make new best friends. After all, I didn't want to be disloyal to my real best friends back in New Orleans. It was kind of confusing.

I also didn't know how long we were going to be staying here and I didn't want to start having all these friends and then having to say "Good-bye, good-bye." I kind of hate good-byes.

Anyway, I missed my old friends. And I missed my old life. Everyone was somewhere else. My two best friends, Sadie and Dana, were in Houston, Texas, and three others were in Atlanta, Georgia. One of my friends went to her grandfather's house in New York, and three others were with relatives in Chicago, Cleveland and St. Louis. We all tried to email each other, but it was confusing and hard to keep in touch. None of us were sure what was going to happen in the next year. I knew from my dad that our house was a wreck, and everyone had a different story.

Sadie and her family had just moved into their house this past May from another house in New Orleans. She was really lucky because her new house was OK, but the house they moved from was totally gone. She still felt upset, because she said that she remembered her whole life in the old house that was now gone, and the new house didn't mean the same thing to her.

I told her that she shouldn't be thinking that way with so many people who had nothing now, and she still had her new house. For a couple of days, we didn't email each other at all. I think that what I wrote made her a little mad at me. But then she emailed me again, and said she knew she was lucky, but what is lucky when so many bad things are happening?

My friend Emma had gone with her family to New York to live with her grandfather. She said New York was amazing, but so big you could get lost all the time. She said there were kosher restaurants all over the place, and more Jewish people than you could imagine. She had seen the Statue of Liberty and said it was "awesome."

I told Emma that maybe my family would come to New York to visit her family and see all the cool things she wrote about. I didn't really know if we could do that, but why not dream? Emma wrote back that her grandfather said that there wasn't enough room in the apartment for my whole family, since as it was, it was crowded with her parents and two sisters in the apartment that was really meant just for one elderly grandfather.

I tried to look back at my email to Emma to see if it looked like I had invited my whole family to stay at her grandfather's apartment. I looked at it and felt you could probably read it that way if you wanted to and then it made me seem really rude, for inviting my whole family over.

But that was the problem nowadays. You try to just be yourself and be friendly and all, but things got mixed up and topsy turvy and

misinterpreted by email, and everyone's getting all huffy with everyone else, even though
we still all want to be friends.

I wished we were all back in our own homes in
New Orleans and just had our regular life back.

CHAPTER EIGHT

A THANKSGIVING TO REMEMBER

The fall went by quickly in Memphis. The weather was cooler than in New Orleans. We celebrated Thanksgiving with Aunt Charlene and Uncle Mike and Sam. My grandparents, Grandma Ellie and Papa Gary, came in from Atlanta, which made things seem more normal. They came in Wednesday night before the holiday and brought us chocolates shaped like turkeys. This was also a family tradition, kind of like the luckshen kugel, only you didn't have to bake it. Grandma Ellie and Papa Gary bought these turkeys at a special store.

Of course, Jonah ate his up immediately. He bit off the turkey's head, and was running around screaming, "Off with his head. Off with his head."

I mumbled thanks, but I saved mine and didn't feel like eating it.

Grandma Ellie noticed right away that I didn't eat the turkey.

She waited till no one else was looking. That's something I like about Grandma Ellie. Even though she notices every single thing, she doesn't make it all into a "big deal" so everyone else knows it too.

"So Gertie," she said, like she was trying to figure out exactly what to say.

But she got right to the point.

"What's with you not eating the chocolate turkey? You always eat it even before Jonah gets to bite off its head."

I wasn't sure what to say back, because of course, what she said was true.

"I don't know," I said, trying to say the truth.

But somehow that wasn't enough for Grammy Ellie tonight. So she continued.

"Gertie, maybe things don't feel the same this year, with all of us being here in Memphis and not at your house in New Orleans."

Uh oh. Something snapped in me. "We don't even have a house in New Orleans." I now was using my shouting voice at Grandma Ellie. And then I made up a lie. "And I'm allergic to chocolate, anyway."

I had heard of kids who were allergic to nuts, especially peanuts, which could make them really sick and not breathe. And some kids even had allergies to kinds of flour, so they always brought their own cake to birthday parties. So why couldn't you be allergic to chocolate too? So that's what I said, because I couldn't think of anything else to say.

Grandma Ellie looked very upset. I didn't think being allergic to chocolate was such a big deal, but her whole face looked like she was going to cry.

"Gertie darling," she said, as she scooped me up onto her lap, which she didn't do as much anymore. Lately it was always baby Sam or even Jonah in her lap. "You don't have to be allergic to chocolate to not want to eat the turkey tonight. Maybe it's just you don't feel like it because everything is different and turned upside down this year. And even the chocolate turkey, which is the same as always, reminds you of what isn't the same."

Like I said, Grandma Ellie knew how to say things right out in a way that wasn't embarrassing to me, like some people, like my mom for instance who always made a "big deal" over every little problem and issue.

I just nodded my head, and then, all of a sudden, I had an idea.

"Grandma, do you want to have a bite of the turkey?"

She looked at me real serious and said, "I would be delighted."

So the two of us sat in the chair and shared the chocolate turkey, just like that. Unlike Jonah, we ate the head last. After all, we were not just five year olds.

Grandma Ellie took me up to bed that night and we read from my newest chapter book together. Then she sang me a song she always sang, using my name Gertie, with lots of words that rhymed and I went to sleep with a smile on my face.

The next day was the actual Thanksgiving Day. On TV, they show the big Thanksgiving Parade in New York City, and I wondered how my friend Emma was doing up there with her grandfather. I wondered if she was able to go out in the snow and see the parade. I wondered if that was now her new family tradition.

Sometimes family traditions can be a pain in the neck. For Thanksgiving, before we actually get to eat the dessert, which includes pumpkin pie, chocolate fudge pecan pie, and apple cranberry pie, everyone has to say what they're thankful for.

Personally, if I was one of the adults, I would have not done this tradition for this year. I didn't think it was a good idea to have to say what you were thankful for when so much was destroyed, disappeared, upside down and gone. But my parents and grandparents apparently did not agree. No not at all.

My dad gave a whole little speech about how this year we had to be especially thankful and grateful for all we had. He then told again his story of what happened with the hurricane. This time, I didn't want to hear it again, so I just got up and pretended I had to go to the bathroom. That is a polite way to show that you are not interested in what an adult is saying.

But even when I got back from the bathroom, we still were not finished with the whole going around thing, because my mom was first and she was going on and on. She was thankful that Dad was OK and that he was able to help so many people. She was thankful that her sister was able to take her and all of us in.

Well, then, my mom and Aunt Charlene got up and were hugging and laughing and then crying too. It seemed to me we might never get dessert. I wanted a piece of chocolate pecan pie and a piece of pumpkin pie too. The apple cranberry could be for someone else.

Aunt Charlene was grateful that baby Sam was growing and doing all of his milestones, like saying "dada" and crawling around. I personally didn't think that his crawling around was something I was thankful for. The more he crawled around, the more he reminded me of Jonah, getting into my stuff and didn't seem as cute as when he just lay there and said "goo." Aunt Charlene was also thankful that we were there because it gave her and Uncle Mike a chance to know me and Jonah better. Well, that was something I could finally agree with.

Now it was Jonah's turn. What would he say? I couldn't be sure he even knew what we were doing, but of course, he had to get a turn anyway.

"I'm thankful," he said and then he stopped and looked around at everyone.

"Aha," I thought. I'm right. He doesn't even know what this is about. "Let's skip his turn," I was saying this just in my brain, not to anyone else. I didn't say it out loud, because my parents would disapprove and strongly disagree and say Jonah deserves a turn like everyone else, but this seemed like a waste of time to my mind.

So then, Jonah looks around the table again, and then he says, "I'm happy that we didn't get a puppy last year for my birthday, even though I really wanted one, because now it would be drowned in the hurricane and dead."

Well, I can tell you, no one expected that from Jonah.

Every one of the adults just kept looking from one to the other.

So I spoke up. "Jonah," I said, "you have rescued this Thanksgiving from just a lot of mumbo jumbo. You acted even older than five years old. You are right about the dog. Now let's everyone eat dessert."

And so we did.

I gave my little speech after Jonah's thanks about the dog because I really didn't want to have to say what I thought about this whole "Thanksgiving theme." Here's what I would have said, but I didn't want to tell everyone, so I was glad that Jonah's talk was the last one.

I would have said, "I do not feel too thankful on this Thanksgiving. I am happy to see

Grandma Ellie and Papa Gary, but that is all for now. I want to be back in our house and Dad says our house is not really even there any more. I want to be back in New Orleans and Dad says the city doesn't even have red lights for cars working right, so nobody can know when to stop or go. And that is how I feel tonight."

I knew that nobody wanted to hear that. So I was happy that Jonah said his thing about the dog and then everybody could talk about that and we could eat dessert.

I had two pieces of chocolate fudge pecan pie, and one small piece of pumpkin pie, just for tradition's sake.

CHAPTER NINE

JONAH'S MEMPHIS MISTAKE

Although I thought Jonah had acted really mature on Thanksgiving, just the next week he made me really upset. Jonah is in kindergarten at my school in Memphis, and we see each other sometimes at lunch, where we have the same lunch time as the kindergarten classes.

When I'm in a good mood, I go over to say hi to Jonah and sometimes talk for a minute to his friends there, Nate and Izzy and Molly and Lucy. Anyway, I was feeling really good and Rachel and Hannah came over with me to talk to Jonah. So Rachel says to him, "Jonah, how are you liking your new school here?" and he looks at her funny and says, "I love school here. I always go to school here."

Uh oh, I think.

So Rachel says, "But Jonah, what about New Orleans? Don't you miss it?"

And Jonah looks at her and says, "I'm not from New Orleans. I'm from Memphis." And all the kids at his table agree, saying, "Yeah, we're from Memphis."

I just look at Jonah with angry eyes and say to Rachel and Hannah, "Let's go. These guys are too little to know what they're talking about." But inside I was really freaking out that Jonah maybe forgot that he was from New Orleans.

I brought it up that night with Aunt Charlene.

"I don't think Jonah forgot he's from New Orleans," she said after thinking it over for a bit.

"I think he just wants to be like the other kids, and the other kids are all from Memphis, so it's easier to say he's from Memphis too."

"Well he's wrong!" I said, very emphatically, maybe a bit too loudly. "And someone has to tell him. NOW."

"I don't know," said Aunt Charlene, her finger kind of leaning against her cheek. "I don't know. It just might be OK for now for Jonah to feel like he's from Memphis. After all, YOU know where you're from. It may be too hard for him for now."

So just like that, I had to accept that now only I knew that I was from New Orleans while Jonah could say he was from Memphis. But that's the way it is. Life just isn't always fair. And now it was getting weird too.

The weirder thing was that my parents were also having some "issues" about being from New Orleans. Or more exactly whether we should return to New Orleans.

The last time my dad came up to see us, I could tell that he and mom were being annoying with each other. I could tell, because I know when I'm sometimes like that, and the feeling is yucky. Also, one night when Dad was in Memphis and I couldn't sleep, I went over to their room and knocked on the door, and before I could get there, I heard their voices louder than usual.

"Marc," I heard my mom say, "I just don't know if I can do it. I just don't know if I can put everyone into a trailer to live. And I just don't know if the air is safe for them. Or whether the schools are going to really be open. I don't know………."

And then I heard Dad's voice, "Jill, you need to know I just can't be running back and forth like this forever. I need you and the kids with me. And they really need me in the hospital. Very few physicians have stayed and there's hardly anyone who can do my work for me. And people won't stop having glaucoma just because there's been a hurricane..."

Knock, knock. I didn't want to hear any more. This was grownup talk and I wasn't sure how to interpret it or who I was for or against. So I just started knocking loudly on the door. Knock, knock, knock.

Mom opened the door. Her face looked a little like she was she had just woken up from a nightmare or something like that.

"Hi Gertie," she said. "What's up?" I thought her voice sounded tense.

I was going to talk to her about not being able to fall asleep, but instead some other ideas just came tumbling out of my brain.

"Mom, why are you and Dad fighting? And why can't we go back to New Orleans? I don't want to stay here in Memphis. And we'll be OK. And I'll help you with Jonah. And we can breathe just fine and we're healthy. And living in a trailer will be an adventure, and you always say we should try something before we say we don't like it."

"Whoa, slow down sunshine." That was my dad talking. "What's going on here?"

"Well, what's going on here?" I asked. Which I thought was a good question.

"Fair enough," said Dad. "Mom and I were talking about what's going to happen next for our family. There's been news that some schools are going to be reopening in January. Also the government is offering to provide trailers for families to live in while we see what we can do next about finding a place to live. And your Mom and I are just trying to decide what's the best way to make a decision as to when to go back to New Orleans."

Mom added, "Or whether to go back."

"What?" I said. "What do you mean?"

Mom explained that some families were deciding not to go back to New Orleans. They were worried that there might be other hurricanes in the future. They were worried that it would be very hard to find a nice new place to live if their house was destroyed. They were worried about finding schools and doctors for their kids.

Well, I understood all that, but I explained to Mom and Dad that we were a pioneer family, just like the American pioneers in the west in the 1800s, just like the Jewish pioneers in Israel in the 1930s, and we were going to have to return to New Orleans. Our trailer would be like the old covered wagon. It would be fun. And that was that.

Mom and Dad thanked me for my ideas. Then Dad went and sat with me till I fell asleep.

I hope I had cleared things up for them and explained to them the right thing to do.

I think I did, because in the morning, there wasn't any of that annoying talk between them. They seemed smiley and cozy again.

CHAPTER TEN

THE TALENT SHOW

The school in Memphis was having a talent show for Chanukah. I wanted to try out and sing, even though I hadn't had any voice lessons since we arrived in Memphis. But as my mom said, "The hurricane didn't take away your voice. That's a gift you can take with you anywhere." So I decided to try out for the talent show.

It turns out that in Memphis these talent shows are a big deal. Lots of the kids want to try out, some as individuals and some do it in groups. I wasn't going to do it as part of a group. I just wanted to get up by myself and sing one of my songs from Louis Armstrong.

My new friends Hannah and Rachel were doing a dance together. They called it "The Dance of the Dreidels," and said it was like the

Nutcracker Suite ballet, with the same music, but with a Jewish theme. They had asked me to be part of it, but I said I had wanted to sing my own song. I think they were a little hurt. They didn't talk to me much at lunch that day.

"Why aren't you talking to me?" I finally blurted out to them. I'm not always so bold, but my Dad has always said that if you really want to know the answer, just ask the right question. So I did.

"Why do you want to do your song alone, rather than dance with us?" Hannah replied. "After all, you can always sing by yourself, but this is your only chance for us to all dance together as dreidels."

I didn't really have a good answer. I just knew that I wanted to sing. My song felt important to me, kind of like I was standing up for something, although I wasn't really sure what.

I hate it when I can't come up with a really good answer to a question that someone asks me, so I had to think a lot. I told Hannah and Rachel I would think about it, but I knew I had to sing my song.

I decided to ask Aunt Charlene, because she was pretty good about these things. What did she think? Aunt Charlene listened to everything and then she said something kind of interesting.

"You know, Gertie," she said, "maybe the answer is in the song you've decided to sing. And in Jonah pretending he was from Memphis."

"What are you talking about?" I asked her. Sometimes, it took a while till Aunt Charlene could translate her good ideas into something I understood properly.

"Well," she started again. "I think it's about the Chanukah holiday."

"Oh brother," I thought. "I don't think this is going to be helpful. My song, "What A Wonderful World" was NOT about Chanukah. Louis Armstrong wasn't even Jewish. But I listened anyway, out of respect for my aunt.

"When I think about Chanukah, it's about the Maccabees having to be brave and take a stand for their own identity, their identity as Jews. At the time, they were being ruled by the Greeks, who didn't want them to be able to practice their religion and have a Jewish identity. So the Maccabees fought back, and well, you know the rest of the story."

Sometimes, Aunt Charlene does that. She says, "Well you know the rest of the story," but it ends up like a mystery puzzle and you have to figure out what she means or where it's going. So I sat for a bit and just stared out and tried to think what the Greeks and the Maccabees had to do with my talent show in Memphis, Tennessee.

And then, bingo, it hit me. "So," I said, now excited and having figured out the puzzle, "I'm a New Orleans Maccabee, and I don't want to stop being Gertie from New Orleans just because we're here in Memphis. So I want to sing my Louis Armstrong song, because THAT is my New Orleans tradition. It's my sign, like the rainbow is a sign, of me being Gertie from New Orleans."

And then I gave Aunt Charlene the biggest hug.

And she gave me the biggest hug back.

Then I had another idea. I wondered if you were allowed to be in two acts in the show. I wondered if I could sing my New Orleans song and also dance The Dance of the Dreidels with Hannah and Rachel.

"Good thinking, Gertie," Aunt Charlene said. "Why don't you ask them at school tomorrow?"

Which is just what I did. And guess what. The answer was yes, that you could be in two talent acts, if at least one of them was considered a "group act" which of course The Dance of the Dreidels was.

I didn't try to explain the whole Maccabee thing to Hannah and Rachel. I just told them the good news that I could try out to sing my song and also to do the dreidel dance. We all spun around in a big group dreidel twirl.

The day of the Talent Show tryouts arrived and I was very nervous. I figured I was doubly nervous because I had to try out two times. My stomach was filled with butterflies, which my mom said always happened for her before big events too. It was funny, because having a stomach with butterflies was something I brought with me from New Orleans.

Tryouts were after school, and I couldn't eat my lunch, not even the pizza, which was really my favorite lunch. At the tryouts, you listened to all the other kids while you were waiting for your turn. And even though it was interesting, it also made my stomach jump a lot. I heard kids singing, saw kids dancing, listened while kids played the piano, the clarinet and even the bells. My friend Joey did a ventriloquist act, and two girls I was friendly with, Aviva and Sarah, did a magic show together.

Finally came our turn to do The Dance of the Dreidels. You see, the music was on a CD from the Nutcracker Suite ballet, but we were dreidels dancing at a Chanukah Party. Once the music started, I began to concentrate on our steps and wasn't thinking about my nervousness any more. It was fun twirling and jumping and acting like real ballerinas. When we finished, we all did a group hug. We wouldn't hear whether we got accepted into the show till the next day.

I still had to wait to do my tryout for singing. Finally it was my turn. Of course, I was kind of scared, but I gave it my all. I tried to remember what my mom had said. The hurricane didn't take away my voice. The teacher who was doing the auditions, Ms. Chassman, was pretty nice to me. "Wow!" she said after I sang. "I guess the music of New Orleans really got into your soul." It sounded like a big compliment.

In any case, the next day I found out that I was accepted into the talent show. For The Dance of the Dreidels. And for my song. Now I was beginning to feel lucky.

I rehearsed every day for the next two weeks. Each day I had to do two kinds of rehearsals, one for dancing with my friends and one for singing. I didn't think about anything else at all.

My brother Jonah complained to my parents about my singing so much, but they supported me this time. They told Jonah that I needed to practice for the Talent Show and that he could go into another room. This was one of the only times that I felt that I got something good out of the hurricane. That is, my parents supported me and my singing and didn't give in to Jonah. That was pretty nice, I thought.

The dance rehearsals were fun too, but very tiring. And we got into a little bit of a fight about what the costumes should be. Hannah thought the dreidels should be blue and white, like the flag of Israel. Rachel thought they should be golden, like the Chanukah menorah. I agreed with Rachel, totally, because I thought the golden dreidels would be prettier, but I didn't want Hannah to be mad at me for siding with Rachel.

So we each put two papers, all folded up, into a bowl, one which said "Gold" and one which said "Blue" and then we each got to pick out just one paper. We would see which color won.

Rachel picked out the paper which said "Gold" even though she really wanted blue. Hannah picked out the paper which said "Blue" even though she really wanted gold. I was next and nervous.

I picked the paper which said "Gold," and so it was. We would be gold dreidels. Hooray. But then I saw that Rachel seemed upset. So I wasn't as happy as I thought I would be. So I said, "What about if we're gold dreidels, with blue trim?" And that is how we decided the costumes, without too many problems.

When I told Uncle Mike about the costume story, he said that he wished people who were leading countries would figure things out the way Hannah and Rachel and I did. And then maybe the world would be a more peaceful place. And that was really nice to hear. It also made me think that maybe I should consider that kind of job for when I was a grown up, if I didn't become a singer or a doctor.

The talent show was two days before Chanukah. My parents said that they would both try to be there, but of course you could never tell with my dad. Uncle Mike said that he could come also and videotape it so my dad would be sure to see it. That was really nice of him, but I still was upset that I could never know till the last minute if my dad was going to show up to anything, including important things like my birthday or the talent show.

Before the hurricane, of course, my dad couldn't come to everything either. He's an ophthalmologist and takes care of people's eyes. But even though he was always pretty busy, he was able to come to my most important events. But now even that wasn't for sure.

The day of the talent show arrived. Dad said he was trying to get to the Talent Show, which was called for 7:00 pm in the evening, but it would depend on traffic. That's how life was and I just had to hope he would get there, but also at the same time, know that if he didn't get there, life would still go on. It was very complicated, but my brain seemed to be adjusting to that.

Joey did his ventriloquism act and everyone loved it. His doll's name was Latke, which was funny, because that's also the name of the potato pancakes you get to eat on Chanukah. Latke sang songs about latkes, which made every one laugh hysterically. Joey also made Latke count all the candles on the Menorah while drinking a glass of grape juice. Joey and I were good friends now, and I was happy his show was so successful.

Aviva and Sarah did magic tricks which were really cool, including making Chanukah coins appear and disappear, which was pretty amazing. And I couldn't figure out how they did it. I tried to see what they were doing from back stage where I was, but it was very hard to see how someone does a trick from there.

Before we knew it, it was time for The Dance of the Dreidels. It took a minute to get the volume sound of the music right, but then, there we were, in glittering gold, with blue trim, spinning and twirling and dancing like you wouldn't believe. At the end of our dance, people were clapping and clapping. I looked out at the audience, and couldn't see for sure who was there, because of the lights in my eyes. I thought I saw my mom standing up and cheering, but I didn't think I saw my dad.

My song was the last thing on the show. I hate being last, but that's the way it is. Life isn't fair. Boy, did I hear that a lot during this year. Blah, blah blah. "Life isn't fair, dear." Well, that was for sure.

But I still wondered why we had to play fair and act fair all the time if life wasn't fair. I reminded myself to put that on my list to discuss with Rabbi Weiss, at our next meeting for the newspaper column.

And while I'm thinking about Rabbi Weiss and the newspaper column, Ms. Chassman comes up to me and says, "Gertie, it's your turn. You're on!"

So without a chance to think too much, which maybe is a good thing, I go on the stage and I start to sing. I sing like I'm a Maccabee and this is my moment.

I open my mouth and the words come flying out, about beautiful trees and flowers, about blue skies and colorful rainbows and about how really great it all is. And while I'm singing, it's kind of strange, but I can feel that I mean every word of it.

And when I finished, you wouldn't believe what happened next! The whole auditorium went wild. Everyone was standing up, which is called a "standing ovation" and clapping and cheering and even whistling. I had never had that happen for me before when I sang. I had seen this kind of reaction on TV for Hannah Montana, but not for me, Gertie.

I couldn't believe everyone was so excited. But I was even more surprised by how I felt inside. I was feeling happy. It was like the words of the song were becoming really true in my own life. Maybe it really could be a wonderful world!

My new friends were here with me, and also some of my family. It was like something was happening to take the sadness out of my heart. I didn't know I could ever feel this way again.

I began to think that maybe I would write songs for people when I was grown up, songs that would make people feel happy when times were tough. Yeah, maybe I would do that.

And while I was thinking about this, suddenly my dad was up on the stage with me! He gave me some flowers all wrapped up and a kiss, and I couldn't believe that I wasn't just in a dream, but that this was real life.

CHAPTER ELEVEN

GOSSIP HURTS

But real life does always come, even after something so amazing like the finale of the Talent Show. That night they announced that I was the number one blue ribbon Winner of the Talent Show. Joey's ventriloquism act was number two. And the girl playing the bells (to all of the Chanukah songs you could think of) won the third place. I was sorry our Dance of the Dreidels didn't win, because I thought we were definitely better than the bells, but like I've said before, life isn't fair.

The only really bad thing that happened is that the next day at lunch, I heard from Hannah and Rachel that Aviva and Sarah (who did the magic show) thought that I had won the show only from the "sympathy vote" because I had escaped from New Orleans. And that if I hadn't come, maybe either their magic show or The Dance of the Dreidels would have won. Now Hannah and Rachel probably should NOT have told me what Aviva and Sarah had said.

They said they didn't agree with Aviva and Sarah and that they thought my song was out-standing." But they thought I should know what some other kids were saying.

Actually, it didn't help me to know what other kids were saying. It only made me feel sad and mad and not have the chance to enjoy my being Number One in the Talent Show as much as I would have liked.

Well, I guess what I learned from that is that it isn't always so friendly to tell your friend something that another friend said about them, even if you think it's a great idea. I can tell you from my own experience. It wasn't a good idea at all.

Chanukah came and went. My parents bought me a new menorah, where you got to use real oil instead of candles for each light. I really liked it and knew that it was a very grown up menorah, but I still missed my old menorah, which looked like a girl or boy Maccabee was holding up each candle. I kind of wanted to see those Maccabee kids again and tell them the whole story about me being a Maccabee girl from New Orleans.

CHAPTER TWELVE

MOViNG BACK HOME, FiNALLY

In January, we moved back to New Orleans. Even though I didn't like doing it, I had to say my good-byes. I had to say good-bye to Aunt Charlene, Uncle Mike and Sammy. Recently, Sammy had taken to following me around and I kind of liked it. So it was sad to say good-bye to him. And before we left, I made sure that Mom got Aunt Charlene's recipe for the chicken with the barbecue sauce, because now I like that too, and I was worried I would miss it when we were back in New Orleans. And I asked Uncle Mike if we could please take the Uno and Candyland with us. I promised I would play Candyland with Jonah, and Mom or Dad would play Uno with me, so I would think about Uncle Mike too.

Then I had to say good-bye to all the new friends I had made. And also to Rabbi Weiss, Morah Moscowitz and Ms. Chassman. Hannah and Rachel and I had a sleepover good-bye at Hannah's house, where we put on the CD of the Nutcracker and did one final Dance of the Dreidels and promised each other that each year at Chanukah we would remember The Dance of the Dreidels.

And I took everyone's email addresses, even though I knew it wasn't exactly the same as being there in person.

It was Monday, January 16th to be exact, on Martin Luther King Day when we arrived back in New Orleans. We had studied all about Martin Luther King in third grade, and I wondered what the Reverend King would be thinking about all that had happened since Hurricane Katrina. You see, when the news reports came out in the days and weeks after the storm had passed, it turned out that lots of very poor black families had been stuck in New Orleans, with no way to get out of town. No cars, no buses, no way at all. Many of these families had suffered really bad things, with some people drowning or starving or getting really sick. I think that Reverend King would have done something to make sure that everybody got help to get out of town, no matter what the color of their skin.

My dad was now working at two different hospitals. My mom teaches math in high school, and her school hadn't reopened yet, so she wasn't sure what would happen with her job. In the meantime, she was helping out at the Jewish Federation with the volunteers who were now coming down to New Orleans to help all of us.

My mom would speak to the volunteers, and take them to see the synagogue (where fish had been swimming in the main sanctuary), the Baptist church which had also been destroyed and our neighborhood, which now looked like some old movie where aliens smashed everything in their path.

At first, I wasn't so happy about all the volunteers coming. "What can they really do?" I wondered. Everything is a mess, and it would take a lot more than some volunteers to fix things up around here. My mom said that the volunteers were amazing.

Students, old people, young people and middle aged people were coming to New Orleans from all over. They were cleaning out houses and rebuilding them, bringing food to old people who still couldn't use their kitchens or get out, and helping to clean up and repair schools and churches and synagogues. They were really making a difference, helping each of us, one person at a time and helping themselves also to be better people. She said there was a story about some starfish she wanted to tell me. I wasn't interested. "Maybe another time," I told her.

The strangest thing about moving back to New Orleans was that we now lived in a trailer parked in the driveway of what used to be our house. Living in a trailer is like nothing I have ever done. It's like one big long room, and everything can be something else. So our kitchen table is also our desk for school work. Jonah and I share a bed that folds down from a wall at one end of the trailer, and my parents have a bed at the other end of the trailer. The bathroom is so small it feels like you're in an airplane all the time. Ruined stuff from our old house sits on the curb by the street, waiting to be picked up by the garbage collectors. Before the hurricane, garbage was picked up every Tuesday and Friday mornings, but now, my dad says the garbage might be sitting around for a couple of months. I mean, who ever really thought that you were LUCKY when your garbage was picked up?

In the meantime, the stuff all sits on the curb and spills on to our sidewalk. My mom said not to touch the garbage, because there's mold and maybe you could catch a disease or something. But a couple of times when she was busy, I did go look and saw a few things I thought I needed. My old Scrabble game was there, with the box top all torn up, but I could see the letters S-C- R-A and I knew what it was. Anyway, I saw a couple of letter tiles from the game and thought I might want them sometime, so I took them (three Es, two Ss, two Ts, two Hs, N, G, K, R, A, O and luckily, J, X and Q, but no U). I put the letters in a plastic bag and keep them with my schoolbooks. When I'm bored in the trailer, I try to figure out what words I can make with the letters I found. I can write my name GERTE (almost like Gertie), and also my brother's name, JONAH (spelled correctly). I can also spell QEEN (with no u).

I also saw one of my Barbie dolls in the trash pile, and that upset me more than anything. It was really dirty and covered with slime and one arm was pulled off. I wasn't sure what to do, but it made me cry. I told my mom and we decided to wrap her up in some gift wrap we found in the trailer and bury her in the backyard. I said the "Sh'ma" prayer because I knew it by heart. And then I sang "What A Wonderful World," although while I was singing I was also crying.

Chapter Thirteen

Another New School

The Jewish Academy had flood damage from Katrina and wasn't going to be opening till September, so I went to our local public school, PS 42, also known as Louis Armstrong Elementary School. My good friend Sadie had also returned to New Orleans and we were in the same class, along with kids we didn't know from before, including Amber, Ava, Malia, DeShawn, Joshua and Elijah. Our teacher, Mrs. Stein, said our class was just like the dream of the United States that Dr. Martin Luther King had spoken about, with black kids and white kids and Asian kids and Hispanic kids all being together, with kids from every religion and every culture. She said we could learn a lot from each other.

Sadie and I became good friends with Amber. She lived with her mom and her brother in a trailer. Her dad was a solider in the US army, and was serving time in Iraq, and she hadn't seen him since the hurricane. Her mom was a police officer and we traded stories about our parents being heroes. We understood each other and shared our secret thoughts.

By February, Grammy Rose was back at the nursing home at Willow Wood and we were going every Wednesday to call out the Bingo numbers. Sometimes, Amber would go with us. Grammy Rose still said that I was her lucky girl. I was still trying to figure out what being lucky meant.

The Sunday before Purim, there was a giant Purim costume party and carnival at the Jewish Community Center, with lots of booths, and cotton candy and a magician. I asked Amber if she could come to the carnival. Amber's family went to the A.M.E. Church on Sunday mornings, but her mom said that she could come to our carnival when their church services were over. Amber, Sadie and I all dressed up as police officers, and we borrowed some stuff from Amber's mom, who was really nice about it.

Once when I went to visit Amber in her trailer, I noticed that she didn't have any books. She said that she always got her books from the library, but now the libraries weren't open. I thought about the Lemony Snicket books I had taken with me to Memphis. And then I realized that it was true, I still had them with me, as the library still hadn't opened.

I talked to my mom about it, and she told me that the libraries had lost thousands and thousands of books from the hurricane. There were almost no books left for people to read. I was really upset. It felt like everywhere something else was a problem. The street lights weren't working. The garbage wasn't being picked up. And now there would be no books in the library. What was the point of a library with no books?

Amber and I decided to talk to our teacher, Mrs. Stein about the library problem. Mrs. Stein thought it was really important. She said that next week she would get the whole class to talk about it for a while. Everyone would get to say their idea. Mrs. Stein called it "brainstorming."

CHAPTER FOURTEEN

MORE GOOD-BYES

My Barbie's funeral wasn't the only one we had to attend back in New Orleans. The Sunday after Purim, our whole family went to Ahaves Shalom cemetery. It's really old, and I had only been there once before, when my great grandpa Aaron, Grammy Rose's husband, had died. I didn't remember it too well. Usually, you bury dead people at a cemetery. But this time, we were burying the Torahs that had been rescued from Beth Israel last September.

Even though we had seen the brave rescuers carry the Torahs out of Beth Israel, it turned out that they were already ruined by the rains. The parchments had gotten soaked, and the scrolls turned into a kind of mush. When something holy like a Siddur (prayer book) or Torah scroll is ruined, it has to be buried in a cemetery, just like a person's body, my dad explained.

After the Torahs were rescued during the hurricane, a Christian woman who worked for the synagogue drove into New Orleans in the middle of the storm to take the Torah scrolls to her house. Within days, she realized that they had been totally destroyed by the water of the storm. According to Jewish law, they should to be buried, if possible, in a Jewish cemetery. But it was impossible to bury them at the Jewish cemetery in New Orleans, because it was flooded and the city was closed.

So this woman took a shovel and dug a huge hole in her backyard by hand, big enough for seven Torahs. And she dug and dug and dug, till the hole was big enough for all of them.

And now, on March 20, 2006, the cemetery in New Orleans was dry enough to properly bury the Torahs there. So we all were there to see something we had never before seen--- a ceremony to bury the Torahs which had been destroyed by the floods.

Because I'm short, I got to go to the front of the crowd and see the big hole at the cemetery. I felt very sad. But one of the rabbis who spoke said something pretty interesting. He said that although the Torah scrolls were being buried, the words that were on them would go on living forever. And that the children would be the ones to make sure that the words of the Torah continued, even though the Torahs themselves were being buried. And I suddenly realized that I was one of the "children" the rabbi was talking about. That was awesome.

I promised myself that I would follow the words of the Torah forever. I would try to see if I could figure out a way to do good things for people, and help make the world a better place, just like the Torah teaches.

CHAPTER FIFTEEN

A GREAT NEW IDEA

On Monday, Mrs. Stein remembered that we would do the brainstorming session about the libraries of New Orleans. She told everyone the rules, which were that you had to listen and you couldn't tell anyone that they had a bad idea. So here's how it went.

Joshua said that we should all bring in the books we had at home to share with each other in our classroom.

Malia said that she was now buying comic books at the supermarket and reading them and she would lend them out to whoever wanted. She would put up a list that people could sign up for.

Elijah said he would rather play ball than read anyway.

Sadie said that her older cousin from Miami was sending her books that she had already read for Sadie to read.

And after Sadie spoke, I had a really good idea. Actually, Mrs. Stein said that my idea was "brilliant."

I said that each of us could email anyone we knew who didn't live in New Orleans and ask them to send down extra books they had to the New Orleans Public Library. Our class and every other class in the school could get involved. Everyone knew people living all over the place since the hurricane. Atlanta, Houston, Memphis, Baton Rouge, New York, Miami, Chicago... The list went on and on. And if we just asked them, maybe they could send us some books that they had already read. And then, they could ask the people they knew, who could ask the people they knew, and maybe hundreds of books would come down for the children of New Orleans to read. Some people might even ask their local schools, or synagogue or church groups to collect books to send down to us here in New Orleans. I was getting pretty excited by the idea.

We called it "BOLA FOR NOLA." NOLA are the initials for New Orleans, Louisiana, so we made up the words "Books Open Library Action" (BOLA) to rhyme with NOLA.

Mrs. Stein contacted the people at the New Orleans Public Library and found the address where people could mail their books to. Sadie, Amber and I spent our free time writing emails and playing library. We took turns for who would be the librarian. For the first time in a while, it seemed like something good was happening.

I told my mom and dad about BOLA for NOLA and they were really proud of me. Mom said that she had told me back in Memphis that I would figure out a way to do good things for other people. Mom told Aunt Charlene, who sent three boxes of books she collected at her synagogue.

Mom said it was definitely time to tell me the story of the starfish. She said she tells it to all the volunteers who come down to help out in New Orleans and now Sadie, Amber and I were amongst the volunteers. This time, I said OK.

So here's the story of the Starfish, which my mom told me, because I wanted to follow the ideas of the Torah about helping other people and making the world a better place. My teachers call this tikkun olam.

One time, there was a girl (my age) walking along the beach and thousands of starfish were washed up on the sand. The starfish needed to be in the water, where they can breathe. On the sand, they would eventually die.

So the girl began picking up the starfish one by one, and placing them carefully back into the water, so that they would live. A boy came by and asked the girl what she was doing. After she explained, he said to her, "But there are thousands of starfish on this beach! There's no way that you'll ever be able to save all of them. What you're doing won't make a difference."

The girl looked at him and thought for a while. Then she replied, "I know I can't save all of them. But I also know that what I'm doing does make a difference. It makes a difference to each starfish that I am able to put back into the water."

When my mom finished telling the story, I was hugging her and crying at the same time. I thought it was a good story. I took out my reporter's notebook that I brought back with me from Memphis and wrote the story down. I thought it might help Rabbi Weiss one day when he needed to explain something to someone like me.

CHAPTER SIXTEEN

A PASSOVER SEDER LIKE NO OTHER

It was April and Passover was coming. Mom and Dad were deciding whether we should go to Atlanta for the holiday to be with Grandma Ellie and Papa Gary, or whether to go to Memphis to be back with Aunt Charlene and Uncle Mike. I brought up my idea that we could stay in New Orleans.

"In our trailer?" Mom asked me, kind of skeptical.

"Yeah, why not?" I said back, a little smartly.

"Well, you know we usually all get together with family, so how would we exactly do that in our trailer? And it won't be so easy to get kosher food and Haggadahs and everything else that we need for the Seder. What are you think-ing, Gertie?"

Well, here's what I was thinking. First of all, our family could stay in the same hotels in town that the volunteer people were staying at. And also, all those volunteers wanted to bring us something, maybe they could bring down a couple of Haggadahs, which are books that tell the Passover Story. Now for a Seder plate, that was not a problem. I had been making Seder plates since preschool, even before kindergar-ten, and so for sure, Jonah and I could get one put together.

And Aunt Charlene could cook the food up in Memphis and bring it down in the car, along with Uncle Mike and Sammy. And Grandma Ellie and Papa Gary could bring along some nice matzahs to eat and afikomen presents, too.

So that's what I was thinking, and that's ex-actly what I told Mom and Dad.

So Mom and Dad sat there looking at each other, and finally, we all did a high five, and they said, "Yeah, let's see if we can have a New Orleans Seder. We went on an Exodus, and now we're back." High five. OK.

So that's how it happened that we were hav-ing the Seder at the Hilton Hotel the second night of Passover. The first night we were all together in this HUMONGOUS community Seder that had been set up by donations from volunteers from all over the United States. It was pretty cool, but there were lots of people and I didn't get to say the Four Questions the way I wanted to, because there were maybe two hundred and fifty people there and lots of them were kids and we all said the four questions together.

So for the second Seder we were at the hotel where our family was all staying together. Even Grammy Rose was able to be with us for the Seder! Just like I had said, Jonah and I made Seder plates. And just in time for Passover, we got a surprise package in the mail. It was a really nice matzah cover that was sent to us by a boy named Solomon from New York, who used money from his Bar Mitzvah presents to buy lots of matzah covers for families in New Orleans. Now that's a nice boy, I thought. If I'm ever up in New York, I would certainly like to meet him!

When we got to the Four Questions, first Jonah got to say the one he knew, and then I did all four of them, in very nice Hebrew, if I do say so myself. But in my heart, I was thinking,

I have many more than four questions for you God. And the questions I have are NOT about matzah and bread, or about dipping vegetables in salt water.

When it was time to dip the parsley in the salt water, everyone remembered the story from when I was Jonah's age and we had been to Aunt Charlene's for Passover. When we got home, I had told my Mom, "Please make sure to get Aunt Charlene's recipe for salt water. Hers is the best." Everyone laughed, because salt water is really easy to make and you don't really need a recipe.

But then, Mom said something about the salt water being the tears for all the sad things that had happened this year, and everyone stopped laughing. And that was the way the Seder went. First we would all be laughing and then someone would say something and we would all stop laughing and some of us would even cry.

My turn to cry came at what used to be my favorite part of the Seder. We would play this game where everyone said what they would have taken with them if they were alive at the time when the Jewish people were leaving Egypt. It used to be a really cool and fun game, hearing stuff everyone would take. My mom would always say her mother Gertrude's candlesticks, and Jonah would say something like his Elmo doll. Every year I would say something different.

But this year, when we got to that part, I began to cry. I wasn't sure why, but I just began to cry, even before it was my turn. First of all, no one wanted to go first except Jonah. And he said his Elmo doll, which he had taken with him to Memphis, so he still had it.

Then my mom said "My mother's candlesticks, even though I can't believe I actually left them here when we went to Memphis."

Now the truth was, when we left that morning before Hurricane Katrina, none of us had thought it was a big deal and Mom had left the candlesticks in the dining room, where they always were. That had caused a mighty big problem once the Hurricane came. The first few weeks in Memphis, every time Mom began to think about home, she kept saying "I can't believe I left the candlesticks" till I didn't want to hear about it any more.

But at least when my Dad checked on the house, and went through the stuff that was still around, he found the candlesticks. They were beaten up a bit and dented and the silver had turned a green color, but this was definitely another story in which my dad was the hero. For sure. Forever.

So now it was my turn and I was just sitting there with tears rolling down my cheeks. I was thinking of all the things I had said in the past that I would take, but most of them were gone now. So everyone sat quietly for a while. I guess everyone was also thinking.

And then I knew. "OK," I said. "If I were leaving Egypt, I would take my most important thing with me." Everybody was looking at me now.

"I would take my family."

Boy, was this a good decision. It was almost as good as when I won the Talent Contest. Everybody burst into applause and was cheering and kissing and hugging. By the time we got to eat the matzah, everyone was in a good mood.

Even when we ate the bitter herbs, we had our usual fun time, with people taking turns to see who could eat more of the bitter stuff and cough and turn red in the face. There weren't any more tears or talking about what a "bitter" year it had been.

Our Passover Seder had turned the corner. And I do think it was because of me. My family was pretty lucky that I often knew the right thing to say. And I was pretty lucky too.

Grammy Rose had been right all along. I was a lucky girl.

YOU CAN MAKE A DIFFERENCE!

Would you like to continue the good deeds that Gertie began? You can donate books to people who need them. Or you can start another project to help make the world a better place!

POSTSCRIPT

Over a million books have been donated to the New Orleans Public Library. At this time, the library itself cannot accept more books. However, you can still help the library and the children of New Orleans by donating your books to the following organization:

Better World Books
ATTN: Rebuild NOPL
55740 Currant Road
Mishawaka, IN 46545

Books sent to Better World Books are either donated to organizations that promote literacy, recycled, or sold, and the monies they collect are sent to the New Orleans Public Library Foundation (as long as you put "Rebuild NOPL" on your package).

You can get more information online about what kind of books they accept:

Better World Books at www.betterworldbooks.com

New Orleans Public Library at www.nutrias.org/foundation/donationsfaq.htm

You can also help children and adults around the world by donating books to the following organizations which you can check out online (with your parent's permission, of course):

www.accessbooks.net
This organization sends used children's books to school libraries in underserved school districts in Southern California. They have a great list of what kind of books they are looking for.

www.africanlibraryproject.org
You are encouraged to collect 1000 books (with your friends and school) to start a library for a community in Africa. You can choose whether it is for young children, older kids, or all ages, including adults.

www.bookends.org
Bookends encourages kids to recycle their books by having student run book drives and sending the books to needy schools and organizations.

www.booksforafrica.org
Books for Africa will send your books to Africa to help people there learn to read in

English. Guidelines are available of what they are looking for.

www.cops-n-kids.org

They accept gently used children's books for police officers to give out to disadvantaged kids to help them to learn to read.

www.ecoencore.org

This organization wants to reduce environmental waste, and they sell the books you send to them and the money goes to fifteen environmental organizations.

www.booksforsoldiers.com

You can sign up to be a volunteer to send care packages to soldiers, which can include books for them to read.

Just like Gertie, YOU can make a difference.

If you want to collect books, or do another project to make the world a better place, you need to have a project plan.

1. Do some research as to what kind of project you want to do and what group or organization you will work with.
2. Decide if the project is one that you will be doing by yourself or with others
3. If you need others (from your school, youth organization, or synagogue or church group) come up with ideas as to how to get them involved.
4. Find out if you will need to raise any money for your project, for example, for buying supplies or for shipping books. If you do, begin to think of fund-raising activities (for example: bake sale, raffle, bowling party, read-a-thon, or dance contest), or use your own money you have saved or earned.
5. Have a planning meeting with your group (or spend time planning by yourself!)
6. Write out a calendar of when each part of your plan will take place.

7. Make sure to have some kind of publicity for your event, whether it's flyers, a story in the school or local newspaper, or online.
8. Keep track of your project in a special notebook.
9. After your event, write about it for the school or local newspaper.
10. Drop me a note telling me about your project.

You can send me an email at:
author@whenthehurricanecame.com

Good luck. YOU can change the world!

GLOSSARY

Afikomen   Matzah hidden at Passover seder; also gift for finding the matzah

Aron Kodesh   Special closet to hold the Torah

Birkat HaGomel   Prayer of thanksgiving after difficult experience

Chanukah   Jewish holiday celebrating religious freedom

Dreidel   Spinning top toy used on Chanukah holiday

Haggadah   Book used to tell the freedom story at Passover

Kugel   Pudding side dish; luckshen kugel (noodle pudding)

Latke   Fried potato pancake eaten on Chanukah

Luckshen Kugel   Noodle pudding

Maccabees   Jewish freedom fighters in ancient Israel in time of Chanukah

Matzah   Flat cracker-like food for Passover instead of bread

Menorah   Candelabra with nine candles for Chanukah celebration

Morah   Teacher

Passover   Jewish holiday celebrating freedom for enslaved people

Purim   Jewish holiday celebrating escape from danger

Rosh HaShana   Jewish New Year holiday celebrated in September

Seder   Holiday meal at Passover where the freedom story is told

Sh'ma   Prayer of belief in God

Shofar   Musical trumpet for Rosh HaShana made of ram's horn

Siddur   Prayer book

Shabbat   Sabbath

Tikkun Olam   Making the world a better place; repairing the world

Torah   Scroll of Jewish law

Tzedakah   Charity

MEET THE AUTHOR

NECHAMA LISS-LEVINSON IS A WRITER AND A PSYCHOLOGIST. AFTER HURRICANE KATRINA FLOODED THE GULF COAST, SHE WENT DOWN TO NEW ORLEANS AS A VOLUNTEER TO HELP REBUILD THE CITY. NECHAMA GREW UP IN NEW YORK AND STILL LIVES THERE WITH HER HUSBAND. THEY LOVE TO READ BOOKS, GO FOR WALKS, HIKE IN THE MOUNTAINS, AND WORK ON PROJECTS TOGETHER TO HELP OTHERS. SHE IS A MOM TO TWO TERRIFIC DAUGHTERS AND CONSIDERS HERSELF SUPER LUCKY TO BE A GRANDMA.